For Samuel — P.F.
For Paddy, Julia and Isabella — J.T.

❀ Note ❀

In Shakespeare's time, girls and women were not allowed to act on stage,
so female parts were played by boys. The apprentice boys would eventually play men's parts,
but while they were young, and before their voices broke, they played female roles.
They often started acting when they were 10-13, and some went on
playing women's parts until their early twenties.

Sam Stars at Shakespeare's Globe copyright © Frances Lincoln Limited 2006
Text copyright © Pauline Francis 2006
Illustrations copyright © Jane Tattersfield 2006

First published in Great Britain in 2006 by
Frances Lincoln Children's Books, 4 Torriano Mews
Torriano Avenue, London NW5 2RZ
www.franceslincoln.com

Distributed in the USA by Publishers Group West

British Library Cataloguing in Publication Data
available on request

ISBN 10: 1-84507-406-8
ISBN 13: 978-1-84507-406-7

Illustrated with ink and gouache

Set in Myriad Tilt

Printed in China

1 3 5 7 9 8 6 4 2

SAM stars at SHAKESPEARE'S GLOBE

Pauline Francis

Illustrated by Jane Tattersfield

FRANCES LINCOLN
CHILDREN'S BOOKS

"There are boats right under our house!" Sam shouted to his mother, the day after they came to live on London Bridge. Sam leaned further out of the window. On the south bank of the river stood a round building with a thatched roof.

"What's that?" asked Sam. His mother came to look.

"That's the new playhouse," she said. "William Shakespeare's plays
are performed there. People say that he's the greatest writer in England."

"Can we go and see a play?" asked Sam.

"No," said his mother. "We haven't got a penny now. You'll have to
look for work here in London, Sam."

Next morning, Sam walked through the hot, narrow streets until
he came to the playhouse.

Over one of its doors was a painted sign. It showed a strong man
holding a globe. The door was open, and Sam slipped inside.

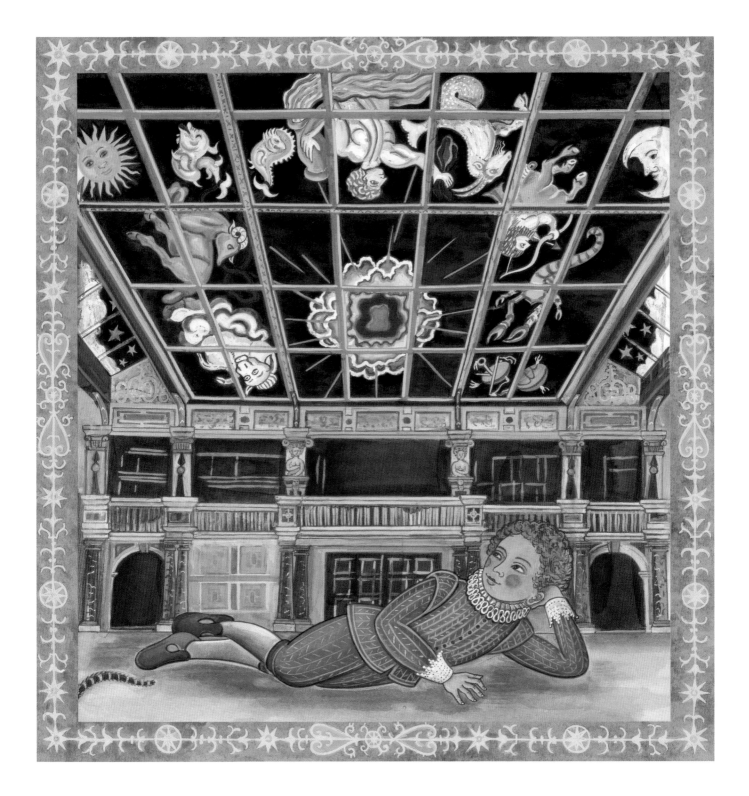

He ran on to the stage, where golden pillars held up a small roof. Sam twirled round and round them until he was dizzy. Then he lay down and gazed up at the painted sky, full of shimmering stars.

It was the most magical place he had ever seen.

"What are you doing here, boy?" asked a voice above his head.

Sam looked up. A man was leaning over the balcony at the back of the stage. The sun glinted on his silver earring.

"I want to work for Master Shakespeare," said Sam. "My mother says he's the greatest writer in England."

"Does she?" laughed the man. "What's your name, boy?"

"Samuel Gilburne."

"Can you act?"

"Not yet," said Sam, "but I want to learn. I can read."

"Go home, lad," said the man kindly. "This stage is only for actors."

But Sam didn't want to go home.

   He opened a door behind the stage and found himself in a large room.
It was full of strange figures: boys with wings on their backs, a short man
wearing a donkey's head, and a tall man muttering,

   " *I, the Man i' th' Moon...*"

A loud roar nearly made Sam jump out of his skin.

"... *Quake and tremble here*
When lion rough in wildest rage doth roar."

It was a lion reading from a scrap of parchment.

The man pulled off his lion's head, put it on the floor and went outside.

Sam picked up the parchment and started to read the words.

All at once an angry voice shouted, "This is supposed to be a rehearsal!
Where is the lion?"

Sam made up his mind: *I'll show them!* he thought. Putting on the lion's
head, he found his way back to the stage. Then he ran on and roared out
his words — until someone caught him and pulled off the head.

In front of him stood the man with the earring. He looked serious.
"You remind me of my son," he said. "He liked playing tricks."

Then he smiled. "You did well just now. I think we can give
you a job here at the Globe, Samuel."

Sam could hardly believe his ears.

"Thank you, sir! And will I see Master Shakespeare?"

The man threw back his head and roared with laughter.

"I *am* Master Shakespeare! Go and ask for a boy called Jack.
He'll tell you what to do."

Sam left the stage in a dream. He was going to work for William
Shakespeare, the greatest writer in England!

"Watch where you're going, boy!"

Sam looked up. A woman was staring down at him. Sam gazed
at the crown on her head. She must be Queen Elizabeth! He bowed.

"I'm sorry, Your Majesty. I'm looking for Jack. Master Shakespeare
says I can work here."

The queen laughed, and took off her hair.

"I'm Jack. I play Titania, queen of the fairies." He grinned at Sam. "Boys play women on the stage. Didn't you know that?"

Sam shook his head.

"We've just started rehearsing *A Midsummer Night's Dream*," Jack explained. "You could play Cobweb, one of Titania's fairies. You only have to say two words and sing and dance. But there isn't much time. The play opens in a week."

On Midsummer's Day at two o'clock, Sam peeped into the playhouse.
Every seat was full. More playgoers stood in front of the stage.
He sniffed the air. Hot meat, garlic and ale. Ugh! He wanted to run home.

The play began. Sam waited and listened.

"Peaseblossom! Cobweb! Moth! and Mustardseed!" called Titania.

Sam danced on to the stage with the other fairies. At last –
he was an actor! He spoke his words loudly and danced nimbly.

He was very pleased with himself.

But the playgoers didn't like the naughty fairies. They hissed, miaowed and even tried to pull off their fairy wings.

"Nobody told me about playgoers!" complained Sam, when the scene ended. "They're horrible! I'm not going out there again."

"Playgoers are like wild beasts, Samuel," said Shakespeare sharply. "It's your job to tame them. Don't ever forget that."

Sam took a deep breath and went back on to the stage.
He danced right up to the playgoers, leaned forward
and pulled a face.

"Mewling maggot pie!" they shouted.

"Tickle-brains!" Sam shouted back.

The playgoers laughed and tried to catch him, but he darted away. He was enjoying himself.

"That's better!" laughed Shakespeare, when Sam came off the stage. "Make the most of it, boy! Not many of my plays are as funny as this one."

Shakespeare's words turned out to be true.

The following week, Sam played a child whose
grandfather, Titus Andronicus, murdered his enemy's sons
and baked them in a pie.

Then he played a Roman boy who watched the
Emperor Julius Caesar stabbed to death by his friends.
    But the part Sam wanted most was the star-crossed
lover Juliet.

One morning, there was great excitement. "We're going to perform *Romeo and Juliet* in three weeks' time," announced Shakespeare, who was carrying a pile of parchments.

The players cheered. Jack laughed at the surprise on Sam's face.

"The playgoers like it because it's a sad love story," he whispered, "and Juliet is the best part that Master Shakespeare has ever written."

Silence fell, as they waited for Shakespeare to give out the parts.

"Jack!" called Shakespeare. "You will play Juliet."

Then he turned to Sam. "You're not ready yet, Samuel," he said.
"You need more experience."

Sam hid his disappointment. He even helped Jack to learn his lines.
But sometimes, when he was alone on the stage, he pretended to be Juliet.

The day before the first performance of *Romeo and Juliet*, Jack was late for the rehearsal. His face was deathly pale and he wouldn't speak to anybody.

"Juliet! Get on to the balcony and speak your lines!" shouted Shakespeare.

Jack began, "O Romeo, Rome... Rom..." and stopped.

"Your voice has broken, Jack," said Shakespeare kindly. "You'll be laughed off the stage if you play Juliet! What do we do? The play begins tomorrow!"

"Sam knows my lines," mumbled Jack.

There was a long silence. Sam's heart beat faster.

"Teach him what you can by tomorrow, Jack," said Shakespeare. "And remember, my players are the finest in all England and the favourites of Queen Elizabeth! We must all work together."

The boys worked hard. By sunset, Sam could walk, talk and dance like Juliet. By the next morning, he was trembling with excitement as he waited for the rehearsal to begin.

The rehearsal started well enough. But towards the end, Sam saw a look of disappointment on Shakespeare's face. What was he doing wrong?

Shakespeare led Sam to the side of the stage.

"When I write," he said, "I have to become the people I write about.

It is the same on stage, Samuel. You must be sad if you want to play Juliet well."

Then Shakespeare told Sam about his son Hamnet – how Hamnet used to play tricks and miss school to go fishing. How, when he was ten, he watched his father act in *Romeo and Juliet*. And how, a year later, he had died suddenly on a hot August day like today.

Sam started to cry.

"Now you will be a fine Juliet," said Shakespeare softly.

At two o'clock, trumpets sounded and a flag flew over
the playhouse. *Romeo and Juliet* was about to begin!

Sam stared in the mirror. He smiled at his reflection,
picked up the hem of his dress and went out on to the stage.

The playgoers sighed when Juliet fell in love with Romeo.
They cheered when she disobeyed her father and married him.
They sobbed when Romeo and Juliet died.
And when the play ended, they stood up and shouted for Juliet.

"Well done, Samuel!" said Shakespeare. "You have made
them laugh and you have made them cry. That is why they come
to the Globe. Now they will go home happy."

"You are the greatest writer in all England!" said Sam.

"Who, me?" laughed Shakespeare.

But he was, wasn't he!